My Cat

Patricia

CANDLEWICK PRESS
CAMBRIDGE, MASSACHUSETTS

For Les, Cliff, John, Colin, Amanda,
and the cats at Wood Green Animal Shelter.

Copyright © 1994 by Patricia Casey
All rights reserved.
First U.S. edition 1994
Published in Great Britain in 1994 by Walker Books Ltd., London.
ISBN 1-56402-410-5
Library of Congress Cataloging-in-Publication Data is available.
Library of Congress Catalog Card Number 93-39669

10 9 8 7 6 5 4 3 2 1

Printed in Italy

The pictures in this book were done in ink, crayon, and watercolor.

Candlewick Press
2067 Massachusetts Avenue
Cambridge, Massachusetts 02140

Jack

Casey

My cat Jack is a

yawning cat.

He's a
stretching-down cat.

He's a
stretching-up cat.

My cat Jack is a scratching

cat.

He's a
curling cat.

He's a lapping

cat.

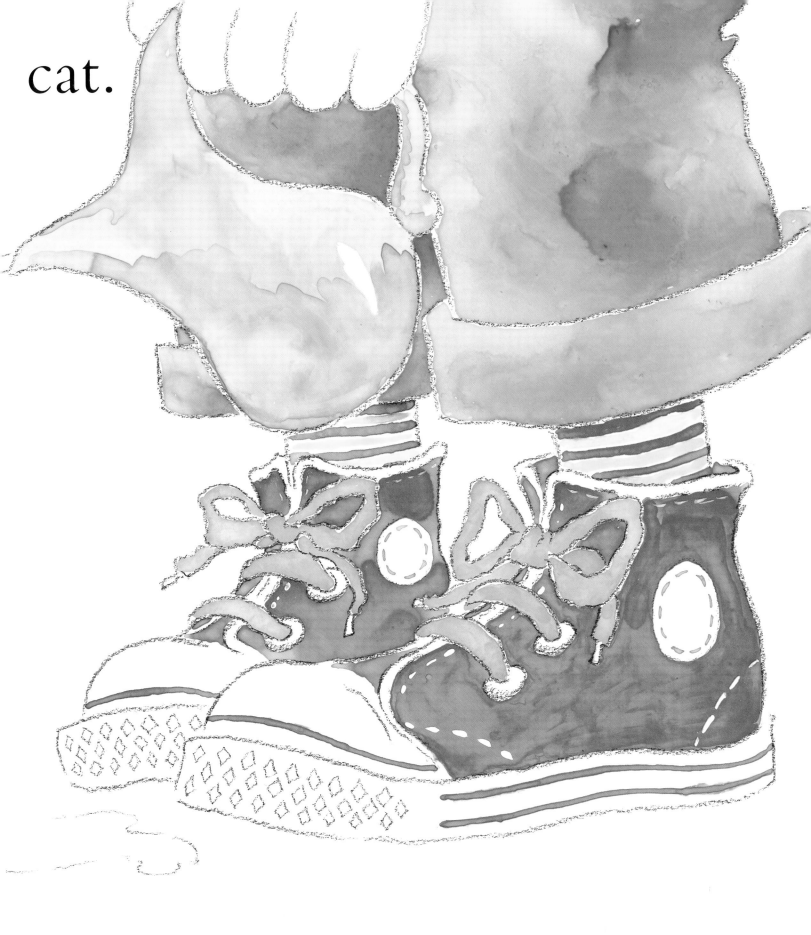

My cat Jack is
 a purring cat,
a rough-tongued cat,
 a washing cat.

He's a
cat who

likes washing
all over.

My cat Jack
is a playing cat.

He's a pouncing

cat.

He's an
acrobat cat.

And sometimes
he's a silly old cat.
I love him,
my cat Jack.

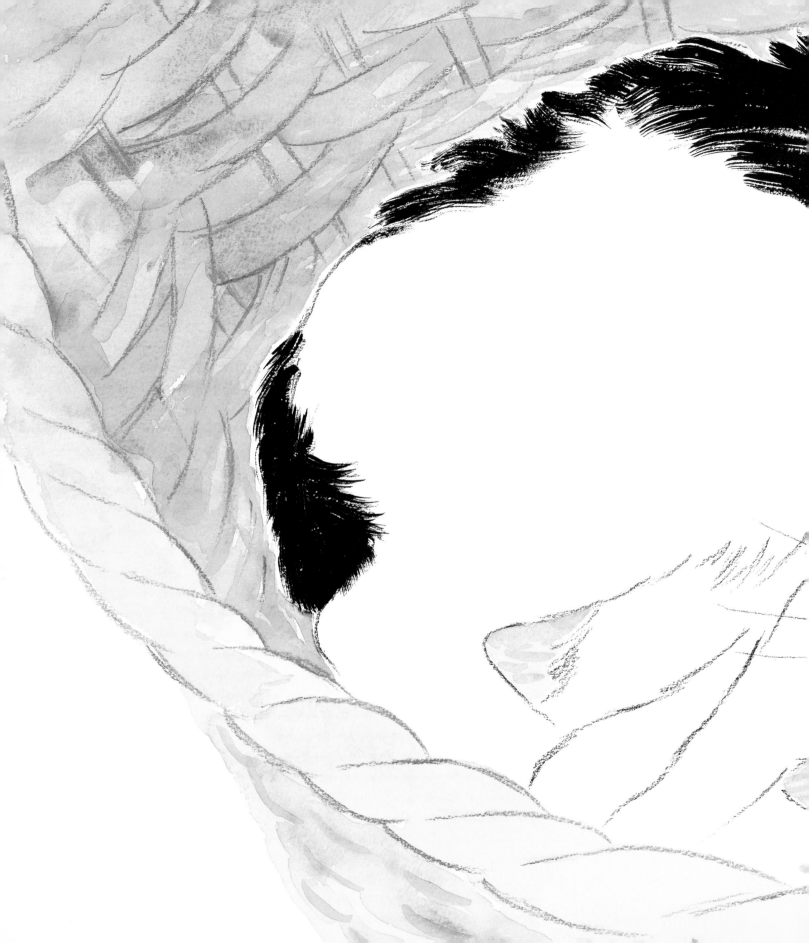